PLATFORM PAPERS

QUARTERLY ESSAYS ON THE PERFORMING ARTS

No. 26
January 2011

CURRENCY HOUSE

PLATFORM PAPERS
Quarterly essays from Currency House Inc.
Editor: Dr John Golder, j.golder@unsw.edu.au

Currency House Inc. is a non-profit association and resource centre advocating the role of the performing arts in public life by research, debate and publication.
Postal address: PO Box 2270, Strawberry Hills, NSW 2012, Australia
Email: info@currencyhouse.org.au   Tel: (02) 9319 4953
Website: www.currencyhouse.org.au   Fax: (02) 9319 3649
Editorial Board: Katharine Brisbane AM, Michael Campbell, Dr John Golder, John McCallum, Martin Portus, Greig Tillotson

Not Just an Audience: Young People Transforming Our Theatre copyright © Lenine Bourke and Mary Ann Hunter 2011

ISBN 978-0-9805632 6 9
ISSN 1449-583X
Typeset in 10.5 Arrus BT
Printed by Hyde Park Press, Richmond, SA
Photo of Lenine Bourke by Melly Niotakis
Photo of Mary Ann Hunter by Robert Clarke
This edition of Platform Papers is supported by the Sidney Myer Fund, Neil Armfield, David Marr, Joanna Murray-Smith, Martin Portus, Alan Seymour and other individual donors and advisers. To them and to all our supporters Currency House extends sincere gratitude.

SIDNEY MYER FUND

Contents

AVAILABILITY *Platform Papers*, quarterly essays on the performing arts, is published every January, April, July and October and is available through bookshops or by subscription. For order form, see page 84.

LETTERS Currency House invites readers to submit letters of 400–1,000 words in response to the essays. Letters should be emailed to the Editor at info@currencyhouse.org.au or posted to Currency House at PO Box 2270, Strawberry Hills, NSW 2012, Australia. To be considered for the next issue, the letters must be received by 10 February.

CURRENCY HOUSE For membership details, see our website at: www.currencyhouse.org.au

Not Just An Audience

Young People Transforming Our Theatre

LENINE BOURKE and
MARY ANN HUNTER

The authors

Lenine Bourke, an Honours graduate in Arts and Education, is currently Executive Director of Young People and the Arts Australia. She has a broad range of professional experience in the arts and cultural sectors, which has taken her throughout Australia and New Zealand, and also to Canada and the USA. She has led arts organizations and projects, and worked for peak bodies, local and state government, statutory authorities, educational institutions, galleries, festivals and artists' groups. These include Youth Arts Queensland, Brisbane City Council, Stylin'UP Regional, Ideas Festival, Backbone Youth Arts, Tafe NSW, the Office for Youth Affairs, Queensland University of Technology, the Roadside Room (ARI), Public Art Agency, Transit Lounge, and Queens Public Girls School (Dunedin). She is currently engaged in various projects with Mammalian Diving Reflex (Canada) in the creation of new performance-based works made in collaboration with children for adults.

Lenine is a skilled practitioner and arts executive who has developed a career across a broad spectrum of art forms and areas such as research, policy development, writing and service delivery. The majority of her work has focused on engaging children and young people, as well as diverse communities. In 2006, Lenine was recognized as a young leader in the industry when she was awarded the inaugural Kirk Robson Award by the Australia Council for the Arts, and again in 2009 when she received the Brisbane City Council Lord Mayor's Creative Fellowship to undertake research in the area of Social Practice. In 2011, Lenine takes up the position of Artistic Director of Contact Inc.

Mary Ann Hunter is Honorary Research Advisor with the Faculty of Arts at the University of Queensland (UQ) and has worked in a range of industry, academic, government, and community settings supporting young people's engagement in the arts. Before joining Arts Queensland to develop its first youth cultural policy and completing a PhD at UQ, Mary Ann trained as a secondary teacher and worked as a theatre-in-education artist. She was a teaching fellow at Nanyang Technological University, Singapore, and a lecturer in the School of English, Media Studies and Art History at UQ, where she was co-editor of the research journal, *Australasian Drama Studies*. She has also been the recipient of various awards and commendations, including the national Philip Parsons Prize for Performance as Research.

Mary Ann has been chair of the Queensland Young Artists' Mentoring Program, a management committee member and adviser on programs such as the Queensland Government's cultural infrastructure program, and has published widely on youth-specific arts and policy, arts education, arts-based peacebuilding, and mentoring. Alongside consultancy work that has taken her from state-theatre archive rooms to remote Torres Strait Island communities, she has been a regular contributor to *RealTime* and a freelance producer for ABC Radio National.

Following a move to Tasmania (via Tokyo), Mary Ann has been enjoying free-ranging with her three under-eights and working with Aboriginal Elders and artists to establish *meenah mienne*, an arts mentoring program for young people in the youth justice system. She continues to collaborate with artists and researchers on the international peacebuilding and arts project, 'Acting Together on the World Stage', and is currently evaluator of the Commonwealth Government's Artist in Residence Initiative. In 2011, Mary Ann takes up a new position as Senior Lecturer in Drama Education at the University of Tasmania.

Acknowledgements

First, we would like to thank the many practitioners whom we interviewed and surveyed about their work, who shared understandings and perspectives on the theatre industry, and who sent us information or clarifications when we requested it. We have endeavoured to reference directly wherever possible, but in particular, we acknowledge the input of participants in YPAA's Blueprint teleconference groups, the National Conversation: Mapping the Future consultation tour, and the Changing Habitats Symposium in 2010. This 'community' of 150–plus people influenced our thinking, and helped strengthen and confirm our direction with this essay. We appreciate your time, generosity, collegiality and inspiring work. We are proud to say your fingerprints are all over this paper.

In addition to these people we also thank some of Australia's youth performing arts luminaries who were particularly generous with their time and advice: Gillian Gardiner, who agreed to be a reader and advisor on the first round of drafts; Tony Mack, who provided feedback on a companion article, which has shaped some of the thinking in this paper; and Rose Myers, who encouraged us in our aim to develop a clear argument about the changing nature of theatre.

We'd like to acknowledge the YPAA Board and the work of YPAA staff member, Imogene Shields, and contractors, Sunny Drake, Kara Beavis, Brooke Newall and Sarah Keating, for providing advice, research assistance and support that freed Lenine to take time out from her role as Executive Director to work on this essay.

We'd also like to thank the director of Currency House, Katharine Brisbane, and the editor of Platform Papers, John Golder, for committing to this work and supporting it through its gestation. Particularly, we'd like to thank John for his ever-gracious feedback, superb editorial gifts, and his encouragement to us to be bold.

Lenine would like to thank Sarah Moynihan, Norm Horton, Warren Gracie, Jane Jennison and Melly Nio Takis for the late-night conversations, reassurance and kindness. Mary Ann would like to thank the young people and mentors of *meenah mienne*; Robert Clarke for survival tea and apple crumble; and Julian, Daniel and Ava for making it all worth it.

Introduction

In August last year, Studio Hair and Beauty in Launceston was overrun by a group of ten-year-olds giving free haircuts. For three days they held razor-sharp scissors to the ears of willing participants and debated the merits of fluoro-favourite colours, patterned buzz cuts, and how to cut to curl. As a feature event of the Junction Arts Festival, *Haircuts by Children* was an exhilarating experience for stylist and styled alike.

This simple act said a lot. Presented by local children and facilitated by Canada's Mammalian Diving Reflex, *Haircuts* was more than a playful act of vulnerability-by-consent on the part of the audience-participants. It offered a study on the machinations of power and generational change. *Haircuts* dared us to imagine how children will manage the future. Will they, Woyzeck-like, role-play to instruction while wielding the razor of power? How will they face the maddening dilemmas? Are they that prepared, and are we that afraid?

Generational change is not a new topic, but it is an urgent one for Australian theatre. We are not talking simply about shifting age cohorts of producers and consumers, but a generationally-defined culture-shift associated with vast technological change and a dramatic increase in Australians' creative arts engagement over the past years. In the present 'culture on demand' world, we can listen to our favourite music, webcast our own mini-dramas, and flex our aesthetic muscles, while realizing our many real and fantasised creative selves on the net. Online we can have a personalized virtual experience of almost any art form, any day, any time—without the hassles of travel, parking, baby-sitting and high ticket prices. Everything is so very immediate. Combined with extraordinary increases in Australia's rate of work participation in the culture industries, it's a heady new era of creative economy partly led by young creatives.[1] The distinction between consumer and creator is being blurred and cultural democracy may just be the order of the day.

So where is live theatre within this explosion of contemporary creativity? How is the Australian theatre sector, with its relatively small and predominantly urban core of artists, engaging with this generation shift? Is it getting defensive by casting the new creatives as culture jammers and nasty competition? Will it retreat into heritage art status? Will it survive by doing what it can to induct kids into theatre conventions while they're at school, in the hope that those same people will become subscribers by the time they meet middle age? Or do current strategies for youth participation implicitly set up the expectation that these potential theatre lovers are going to need to find themselves in urban settings and with the wealth required to attend theatre, to have even a remote chance of developing the cultural capital to make it?

Is this good enough?

This essay is about generation shift, young people and Australian theatre. It's about how young people, children and the theatre artists who work with them could play a key role in making the Australian theatre industry much more than good enough. Prompted by a few recent national events—including the Australian Theatre Forum and the Australia Council Arts Marketing Summit in 2009, as well as some of our own experiences of the youth-specific sector being perceived as 'worthy' but somehow 'less than' the rest—the essay muses on the gains and dilemmas of theatre for young audiences; the creative risks of participatory youth theatre; and the ways emerging theatre artists are being fostered. In particular, it alerts the theatre community to how national and international contemporary youth-specific performance is effectively signposting current issues and future options for the theatre industry as a whole.

Chronologically speaking, the essay comes between two landmark projects: the Australia Council Review of Theatre for Young People, completed in 2003,[2] and the major Australian Research Council Theatrespaces project, a collaboration between Melbourne, Griffith and Sydney Universities and a number of eastern-seaboard theatre companies, which is soon to release its findings on the factors that effect the engagement of young people (14-30 years) in theatre.[3] With respect to these key projects, our essay is less a statistically savvy report card than a work of overview and creative projection. In it we take licence to imagine 'what if ...'

What if the Australian professional theatre community (now populated with its fair share of former youth-theatre participants) finally let go of the outmoded idea that children's and young people's work serves as a stepping stone to the serious stuff of a national theatre industry? What if children and young people were more than a tick-a-box priority? What if the theatre community, as represented by those who attended the 2009 Australian Theatre Forum, acknowledged the ways in which youth-arts practitioners have already cultivated the kind of well-functioning professional support networks that it yearns for? What if it recognized that artists at the leading edge of international and Australian youth-specific performance have a lot to offer adult audiences and can signal vital new trends? And, crazily, what if young punters camped out to get their tickets to the next state theatre show as they might for the next Big Day Out?

What if, quite simply, young people were brought in on the act of transforming Australian theatre? Our aim in the following pages is to explore why and how.

Children and young people get the current generational shift better than anyone else: they're living it, activating it, and they're even making money out of it. When it comes to theatre, they want and deserve great work. And don't believe the myth that they can't sit still or don't get Shakespeare. They just want to be 'more than just an audience'. Despite the image of ipod-clad self-containment, young people generally want to interact. As they become creators, they don't want to compete with or be separated from more skilled, established, or older artists and audiences—good mentoring and training are still essential to cultivating ongoing professions of excellence. But they do want to collaborate, work fairly, and have opportunities to lead and shape and critique. They might like watching, but they would far rather be doing. This may even be more so for regional, remote and economically disadvantaged young people, who simply can't get access to the best our national theatre industry can offer. They are often the ones also struggling to find the means to access a home computer or mobile phone, let alone gain broadband or mobile coverage in their town. How do they get introduced to the imaginative, socially relevant, and fantastical experience that theatre can be? (One answer is that they try to make it for themselves). The pull to create may also be especially true for young people who have responsibilities as custodians of their Elders' and communities' stories, and who every day negotiate complex intergenerational spaces. These young people are vital to the sustainability and growth of their regions and their various cultures. These young people want *into* cultural action, rather than have to wait for one-off tours by visiting theatre artists, tours that more often than not are decided for them by mediating adults and sometimes cautious gatekeepers.

How do we know this? One of us has lived through these changes as a young artist and audience member sitting on the border of the so-called 'Gen Y': Lenine, who is Director of Young People and the Arts Australia, has just returned from a six-week national consultation tour to urban and regional areas to investigate ongoing issues in the youth-specific arts sector. She has also spent time in remote areas experiencing and discussing these issues. And Mary Ann, on the fringe of 'Gen X', has been looking at old ideas anew. Actively involved as a practitioner and policy maker in the field from the mid 1990s, she is an educator, researcher and writer now experiencing the sector in surprising new ways from within a 'family audience' demographic. We have both worked closely with children, young people, artists, educators, and policy makers in a variety of academic, industry and community settings and together started a discussion about these issues around ten years ago. We've talked with over 150 practitioners of the youth-specific arts sector, most recently as part of the national tour and the allied research activity of the 2010 Young People and the Arts (YPAA) National Symposium. And we've seen how these issues have been resonating and converging with international developments in theatre, audience development and arts marketing more generally.

We acknowledge that the term 'youth' has wide-ranging and contested meanings and, to avoid the risk of invoking a simplistic 'new generation' discourse, we do not subscribe to a homogenizing view of young people's interests as oppositional to the mainstream or 'adult' world. We recognize and value the contribution of children and young people to a diversity of contemporary, traditional, conservative, cutting-edge and grassroots performance practices. And we respect that, within the age category of babies to 25 years, interests and needs clearly differ.

However, we believe there is an urgent need to articulate the recurring concerns of theatre practitioners working with and for this age group, as well as those of young people working as artists and arts workers in their own right. At best, they are acknowledged for cultivating the future of the theatre industry, yet they are rarely invited to join in the conversation about current or new directions. Policy lip-service may be paid to building new audiences, empowering creative citizens, and educating young artists, but these practitioners sense a lack a commitment within the broader theatre industry to fostering new-generation leadership—which is interesting, given the role that youth arts has played in the early development of many of our leading practitioners in Australia today. Those working with young people would like to know how the theatre industry is capitalizing on the waves of regional and urban young people skilled in creative enterprise and interaction via their growing up with web 2.0. How is the industry responding now that there's a surplus of eager new creators, but a deficit of new audiences? What to do now that, as a society exhausted by the sheer pace of the 24-hour plugged-in new world order, we are beginning to prefer a good night in to a good night out?[4] Engaging young people more fully in Australia's theatre sector doesn't require a revolution. Small but significant shifts in perspective— triggered by some fresh perspective on the children's and young people's sector, as well as some 'what if' imagination—could contribute to a new sensibility that transforms the now seemingly perennial crisis in which Australian theatre finds itself.

Current factors in the new world order

Over the last five years, the potentially catastrophic issues of climate change and the global financial crisis have impacted on the values and workings of Australian society. During the 2010 federal election campaign, these issues were re-branded and streamed across television, radio and the internet, with claims about government spending, population control, immigration, asylum seekers, jobs and taxes fuelling the debate. When it came to children and young people, attention turned mostly to 'working families' and their struggle with affordable housing, adequate public health care and quality education, alongside the obligatory conservative proclamation that more young people need to be locked up in order to control crime. But, generally, the impact of the global was linked very clearly and very closely to the personal and the everyday.

For the most part arts and cultural issues were sidelined in these debates and political campaigning. While there were persuasive calls for a national cultural policy to be placed back on the agenda—one that acknowledged that a new generation of creators and consumers of contemporary broad-based culture no longer works as their predecessors did—in the hands of the mainstream media this lapsed into a heritage-versus-contemporary arts tiff.[5] Political attention was turned to the arts at the last minute, but this seemed to be about placating voters in the seat of Melbourne who, we now know, were about to make history by electing the country's first federal Greens MP. It seemed that creative communities did have some clout, and that ignoring their needs was not going to be a vote-winner for either major party. The lobbying by 20 national peak arts organizations around election time resulted in some promising collaborations across the creative and cultural industries, however: a positive development for sectors more used to competing for government arts support.

But to return to the global: at the 2009 Australia Council Arts Marketing Summit, US arts manager and commentator Ben Cameron pointed out that global crises have had a very real impact on all sectors of the live performing arts. He described how audiences have eroded due to the high cost of tickets for live arts that are resource and time intensive. Companies are not only struggling with the disappearance of subscribers and audience members prepared to book ahead, but also battling with the challenge of enticing a populace who are simply exhausted by other demands on their time. Debates about government intervention in the arts in Australia have often hinged on the Commonwealth's perceived preference for the 'establishment' end of arts market supply, yet the challenge for the future of our theatre industry is more complex than who gets what from a limited pool of subsidy. The way people value their time and choose to communicate has changed so profoundly over the past decade ... How is the theatre industry responding to this? And, indeed, should it?

A number of important factors need to be considered when assessing theatre's relevance within this changed environment and its connectivity with those who are leading and living this change, namely young people and children. These centre around technology, access, money and cultural authority. In this environment, young people become both an opportunity and a threat: they are undeniably the future of the industry, yet their new ways of interacting with each other and with the world threaten the very legitimacy of the conventional theatre experience.

Factor One

Technology offers accessible and intimate creative participation

Provocateur Clay Shirky, who writes on the economic and social impact of internet technologies, estimates that there are roughly one trillion hours of free time available in the world every year. He argues that in the twentieth century industrialized society created the conditions for people to *consume* in these hours, whereas, in the last ten years, with the explosion of digital technologies, people now have the tools and desire to *create* in this time. Regardless of how 'stupid' or amateur the creations may be, he says, the process is creative nonetheless and 'once they have done it, they can do it again and again and keep improving'. [6] During this improvement cycle individuals begin engaging others, whether it is for 'communal value' (such as 'LOLcats', Shirky's example) or for broader civic value, like the collaboratively initiated web platform Ushahidi, which helps gather data from SMS, email or the web in order to create maps or timelines for public crisis response. [7] Although, as

New Yorker writer Malcolm Gladwell deftly argues, the internet can be overrated when it comes to effective social activism,[8] on the advent of Australia's National Broadband Network (NBN), traditional cultural industries cannot afford to ignore the ways in which people are using the internet and these trillion global hours. The shift from an era of consumption to an era of creation provides a challenge to conventional ideas around why and how we make and market theatre.

For many people, the internet provides a much more 'live' and personalized experience than the 'live arts'. For those of us lucky enough to have home computers and fast broadband access, almost anything we want is available at any time of the day. It was a scenario hardly imagined 15 years ago. We can create art, catch up with friends, watch movies, see TV shows and make video clips. We can publish our thoughts and experiences to the world, document our ordinary and not so ordinary moments and share these via video, written text, sound, photos and digitally created narratives. As Ben Cameron points out, there are now expectations of convenience and personalization that live performing arts organizations—organizations that depend on fixed curtain times, specific geographic venues, attendant inconveniences of parking, travel and the like—simply cannot meet: 'What will it mean in the future when we ask a potential audience member to pay $100 for a symphony, opera or dance ticket, when that consumer has been accustomed to downloading on the internet for 99 cents a song or for free?'[9]

With interactive user-generated web 2.0 applications, the internet now plays a key role in facilitating

creative output. And web 3.0 developments suggest that the web browser will become even more
part-personal assistant / part-friend in a life-stream
approach that is billed to personalize the masses of
data out there even more. We may even be wearing
our PCs as headsets sometime in the future—a great
post-millennium anxiety.

Our aim in these pages is not, however, to instil
fear and anxiety, but to highlight the importance of
understanding how these trends are changing people's
perception of time and their choices in using free time,
and what opportunities these trends present for the
interface between digital technology and the live and
tactile arts.

So, just a few more stats before we talk theatre.

Did you know that Australians were the world's
'biggest users of social media'?[10] Australians spend an
average of 6 hours, 52 minutes per month on social
media sites, 43 minutes more than North Americans,
who spend 6 hours, 9 minutes. And if you think it's
all young people, think again, as Neilsen polls also
indicate that the largest take-up of internet usage in
2008–2009 in Australia has been in the 65–74 age
group, although it has to be admitted that this group
was starting from a lower base rate for participation
in the preceding year. It needs to be said that rates of
use also have a lot to do with access—both access to
computers for private use and access to reliable internet connection. Aboriginal and Torres Strait Islander
people, for instance, many of whom face both these
issues, experience a home-access rate of only 36%
compared with the national average of 67%.[11]

In 2008, an estimated 2.2 million (79%) children (aged 5 to 14 years) accessed the internet either during or outside school hours.[12] And while it is difficult to find directly comparable data around actual time spent engaged in these activities, it is interesting to note that, in the same period, 1.9 million (71%) children aged 5 to 14 years attended a public library, museum, art gallery or performing arts event at least once outside of school hours. This included 913,900 (or 34% of all Australian young people aged 5 to 14) attending a performing arts event.[13] The Australia Council's recent report, *More than Bums on Seats: Australian Participation in the Arts*, a representative survey of 3,000 Australians over the age of 15 years, further demonstrated that

> in terms of creating art online, 16 per cent of all internet users were involved in posting works of art, writing blogs and working with others to create art [...] with 41 per cent of all online creators aged 15–24 years.[14]

The current state of theatre participation makes for a sobering contrast. A costly group-based art, it is, of course, much harder for young people and others to access as creators. And, although the age cohort of young people surveyed by the Australia Council was only 15 to 24 years, the rates of their participation in performing arts compared with the general population were revealing. According to *More than Bums on Seats*, young people's active participation rate in theatre and dance is 17%, yet this drops to an alarming 4% for the general population. Audience figures for theatre and dance are also of concern when they fall from 40% of young people attending a dance or theatre event in the last 12 months to 26% for the general public. This is a big erosion. Why does it seem that young people, once independent of school, and considering their own free choices with their time and income, are choosing to sever their ties with theatre?

It is impossible to draw sound conclusions from these incomparable sets of data on internet use and engagement in performing arts. But a 'drop-off' trend is clear and, generally, while young people are often cast as the problem in declining theatre audience and participation rates, they are rarely invited to lead the search for solutions. The major Australian Theatrespace project will soon address this by providing more detailed evidence of the factors that enhance and impede young people's involvement in theatre (from young people's perspectives). Nevertheless, the immediate challenge for the theatre industry is how to harness this early engagement into better long-term participation and audience rates. The related question that underpins this essay is this: to what extent can new directions be informed by an acceptance of the new creative economy's dissolution of the traditional consumer/creator divide?

Factor Two

Erosion of audiences

Attracting and developing new and existing theatre audiences is tricky business. Subscribers and pre-purchasers are changing their behaviours in response to busier and less-predictable work and social lives. As Cameron and others have observed, this is perplexing for marketing professionals and public relations specialists as they try to motivate a fatigued public. The situation is also challenging for regional venues, presenters and festival curators, as they are left unsure how to sell theatre to regional and remote communities.

School-aged audiences are as surefire a target as any in these testing times. In both regional and urban venues, tickets for young audiences are mostly purchased in group blocks by teachers, sometimes up to 12 months in advance. This makes children and young people not only a reliable tick-a-box priority, but also a highly attractive market segment for the company bottom line. We might well say hooray for young people's theatre, but the matter is more complicated. For, rather than wooing the target audience in these circumstances (the children and young people), any smart marketer / presenter / venue manager is going to woo the purchaser (the teacher or parent)—resulting in a significant warping of the conventional chain of supply and demand. Theatre companies that engage in direct communication with young people are few and far between, so that, when a young person grows out of school-facilitated theatre attendance, there is somewhat of a black hole. What connection do artists, companies, marketers and policy developers really make with young people as they reach secondary school and beyond? What is the incentive for young people to keep attending when the time comes for them to decide for themselves? How do they negotiate this environment, when they have never had the freedom to explore it before? Is the work good enough to keep them coming back?

We are hopeful that there will soon be Australian evidence to suggest that engaging a child or young person as an audience member of theatre will increase the likelihood of their becoming a long-term theatregoer. But even if it is shown that this may well happen, will maintaining the status quo on the basis of probability be good enough?

What we *do* know is that making and marketing work for young people over the age of 13 is really hard work, although stand-out companies like Zeal Theatre in New South Wales, and Real TV and Arena Theatre, both in Victoria, demonstrate that it can be done. In fact, this cohort of audience has become so troublesome to engage that, in 2010, the directors of two of the country's leading festivals for young people, Come Out in South Australia and Awesome in Western Australia, shifted their programming attention away from this group in favour of pre-teens and the early years (under 5). While there may be sound justification for these decisions—and undeniably it's a great development for the growing field of performance for the under-5s—this means that there are now fewer opportunities for practitioners making work for older cohorts.[15] The lack of 13-years-plus programming in state-based arts festivals, youth festivals and touring initiatives creates a significant gap. Are we really so unsure of who these young people are, and afraid that they have so little taste for theatre that we simply stop creating work and opportunities for them?

In terms of marketing and audience development, teachers continue to be intermediaries in the group booking and touring of performances at an age when young people are starting to negotiate their way independently to the movies, sports events and live music gigs. While the price of tickets might be a factor—not that the difference between the cost of a cinema ticket and a concession theatre ticket is that large—could it be that, by marketing to schools as the safest, most convenient and cost-effective route to young audiences of this age, companies are aligning their works too heavily with curriculum imperatives or overtly instrumentalist goals to maintain these key market buyers?

For young people, it's a bit of a raw deal, and for the theatre community it's a wasted opportunity.

Factor Three

Money and jobs

Economically speaking, the arts can be a blur of contradictions that reflect specific values about class, culture, geography and heritage. These contradictions span funding systems and wage and working conditions. For instance, commentators such as Marcus Westbury have highlighted some of the significant discrepancies in subsidies to the Australian arts industry: most notably that, in 2009/2010, Opera Australia's funding from the Australia Council was—according to his analysis of Australia Council's

2009/2010 successful grants list—more than the combined total of all successful individual projects and artists' grants awarded during the same period.[16] With respect to wages, two recent reports on artists' income, led by David Throsby and Stuart Cunningham, indicate that artists earn a median income of $35,900 a year, which includes both their arts and non arts-related income. Of those artists, 16% earn less than $10,000 and 5% earn more than $100,000.[17] So, in Australia, it's something of a truism to say arts funding is tenuous, organizational funding is the norm, and professional artists struggle.

Enter the contemporary new wave of 'amateur professionals': young creatives experienced in and inspired by the creative opportunities afforded by accessible digital technologies and the World Wide Web. In the new world order, the arts are supposedly being democratized as more people bypass traditional education and training routes to professionalization. In a high-cost industry like theatre, will this exacerbate an already significant problem in that established theatre professionals are already doing it tough to maintain a viable career in the arts? Especially if they move to regional home towns?

What Australia lacks is a clear, responsive and visionary national cultural policy that might help to situate and address these new developments. Various state, territory and local governments are doing their best to deliver positive outcomes for artists, communities, and the national cultural account, yet there is little evaluation and even less public disclosure around how strategies are developed in response to contemporary changes in the industry and society. As Ben Eltham and Marcus Westbury have advocated, 'We are a nation that is a creator and not merely a consumer of culture, and [...] Australians are active and enabled participants in the increasingly globalised cultural pool'.[18] Young and emerging artists are central to this policy debate, as is the development of a national theatre ecology that encourages and values the so-called 'small players', like youth theatre participants and practitioners, as much as the bright young cultural exports on the competitive fast track to success.

Factor Four

The apron strings of cultural authority

Lenine's diary, 2009:

> It's May and I'm at the extraordinary Australian Theatre Forum, held at Melbourne's Arts House Meat Market. The event is a national gathering (the first of its kind in over 20 years). It brings together practitioners across generations who work in the theatre industry—including me as an independent artist and as Director of YPAA. We're meeting to share ideas, opinions, issues, and visions for the future.
>
> It's interesting that there are heaps of participants here from youth arts organizations all over the country. Yet, when prompted a little bit to reflect on their experiences, they confide to me in the bar next door just how frustrated, concerned, overlooked and

unimportant they feel. Their opinions and contributions are undervalued because they are perceived to be inexperienced, and 'only working with young people'. They are invisible to the broader industry.

As other practitioners keep lamenting during this gig about how the theatre industry doesn't network very often or very well, those of us working in the youth sector want to disagree—we engage in networking, professional development, resource sharing and, in fact, have had our own peak body for over 30 years. This year alone no fewer than five Australian companies are touring shows for young audiences internationally. We feel organized, proud and strong, but are our contributions sidelined because of the age of the collaborators and audiences we choose, or perhaps because of our own ages ...?

June 2009. The Theatre Forum is over—aspects of it were great, but I am left with a lot of questions about who has the cultural authority in this industry. I'm now at the Australia Council's Marketing Summit and it isn't until I hear Ben Cameron's fucking inspirational speech that things begin to make sense. He says there's been 'an explosion of creativity, a class of amateurs doing work at a professional level' on the internet, in film festivals and dance competitions. He says that 'they're expanding our aesthetic vocabulary' and dares to suggest that 'they are also assaulting our traditional values of cultural authority and undermining our ability as arts organizations to set the cultural agenda'.[19] This is a very powerful statement and gives me the impetus to plan the 2010 YPAA national symposium around the question 'Are children and young people democratizing culture?'—and to write to Currency House with the idea for this Platform Paper. I've seen the previous papers and noticed that young people's theatre hasn't yet rated a mention.

At random moments, current leaders from within the Australian theatre industry can very easily chew up and spit some of their own, and at others they can be the most nurturing and supportive mentors and advocates. The mainstream media continue to give the cultural old guard the final say in debates about national cultural policy and the value of the arts. And so it took someone from the other side of the world to tell a room full of marketers and practitioners that we are frightened—frightened of the young, frightened of the amateurs, and frightened that our positions of power, which are already so tentative, might need to be reconsidered and re-allocated. This shift in power and cultural authority is happening.

As practitioners and researchers of young people's performance, we've been experiencing and thinking a good deal about this shift. We have seen some examples of how it is happening in contemporary Australian and international theatre, and we've noticed signposts within the youth-specific sector that herald interesting new directions for the industry at large. We've also tried to activate in our own ways: Lenine has joined the curatorial committee for the next Australian Theatre Forum in 2011 and Mary Ann has been actively mentoring young practitioners and writing further on recent developments in the field.[20] By framing our own response to the power shifts articulated by Ben Cameron in terms of 'what if', we want to suggest how as a theatre community we might replace this fear with opportunity.

What if ...

the Australian professional theatre community let go of the outmoded idea that children's and young people's work serves as a stepping stone to the serious stuff of a national theatre industry?

Say 'theatre and young people' and many Australians conjure images of ham-fisted theatre-in-education, large-cast collages on teen pregnancy, and Chris Lilley's indefatigable Mr G. While accepting that working with children and young people as artists, audiences or students is important—Australians widely believe the arts should be an important part of the education of every Australian[21]—many people outside the youth-specific sector have little knowledge of the depth and professionalism of this field of practice. The well-worn stereotypes at the centre of this image problem do, however, have their origins in key developments over the past 30 to 40 years, and they are worth briefly recounting here.

British-born Theatre-in-Education (TIE) had a major impact on the growth of professional theatre for young audiences in Australia in the 1960s and 1970s, with expat artists Barbara Manning, David

Young and Roger Chapman leading the establishment of TIE-devoted companies such as Salamanca,
Arena, Toe Truck and Magpie around the country.
Furthermore, companies such as Jigsaw in Canberra,
under the directorship of Carol Woodrow, evolved
participatory educational drama and theatre programs.
Yet, with the comparative limitations of Australia's arts
funding systems, state-based education policies and
costly touring conditions, the strongly interactive ele-
ment of the original British model was lost and many
skilled artist-teachers became mere visiting players
enduring long drives to schools to deliver 50-minute
set pieces in halls and cluttered classrooms. Despite the
significant development of a quality 'writers' theatre'
as a response to these conditions—which at its best
eschewed the didactic temptations of such helicopter
visits—the process of marketing, scheduling and touring to geographically dispersed schools controlled by
centralized state authorities was still much harder
in Australia than in the UK with its closely settled
and relatively independent counties.[22] In the long
run, to maintain cost-effectiveness, actors and actor-
teachers had to become multi-skilled in all facets of
administration and touring—with the result that the
quality of performance deteriorated. Consequently,
working in Australian TIE developed into something
of a rite of passage for young theatre workers fresh
and eager enough to devote long hours for little pay.
It's therefore little wonder it became an entry-level
step-up to better jobs.

But, more than that, the status of TIE, and the more
participatory and socially critical youth theatre that

followed, suffered at the hands of Australia's lingering post-War social attitudes to children as being seen but not heard. Being a theatre artist in Australia was hard enough in the days of the national cultural cringe, but working with children and young people enjoyed even less prestige. You needed to be particularly passionate and/or be a bit of a revolutionary yourself to commit to a career in this sector.

The early work of TIE did have a major impact on the development of youth and community theatre in the 1970s and early 1980s—driven partly by a generation of innovative teacher artists who graduated from Rusden Teachers College in Melbourne (now Deakin University) at around this time. The interconnections between progressivist education, community development and a 'democratizing theatre' were cast. Youth theatre was seen as a vehicle for young people to express themselves beyond the confines of school-based learning, and the collective process of such work empowered young participants to speak up publicly on issues that affected them. With a lot of political urgency but little funding support, over time there evolved a certain 'genre' of youth theatre: the issue-based, earnest, large-cast collage. While youth theatre forms have come a long way since then (as has drama education), the awkward nature and patchy production quality of these early exploratory enterprises continue to plague contemporary perceptions of practice.

In the 1980s and 1990s, agenda-setting state theatres and major adult companies began to develop education and youth arms to their mainstage programs, although these efforts were directed more towards building future audiences than driving innovation in theatre for, with or by young people (although Magpie and Arena, linked as they were to their 'parent' state companies, are worthy exceptions). Innovation was left to struggling small-to-medium organizations that were mostly community-based and often founded on educational or social change imperatives; but with infrastructure and finances too limiting to make any significant mark on the wider professional theatre industry. The work of Patch and Flying Fruit Fly Circus are notable exceptions, but generally it wasn't until the full flight of Adelaide's Come Out festival into the 1980s (it had been established in 1974) and the strengthening of the Australian Youth Performing Arts Association in the same decade that a niche ecology of youth-specific performance practice took shape. Since then, more than five large-scale performing arts festivals for young audiences have gained prominence around Australia. Adelaide has been the only city in the world to host two ASSITEJ international young people's theatre festivals, and contemporary Australian companies for young audiences such as Arena, Zeal, Real TV, Windmill, Polyglot and Slingsby tour internationally and have been the recipients of a range of international prizes and awards.

That working with children and young people in the arts has now become a viable career choice was evident at the 2010 Young People and the Arts Australia Symposium, at which delegates were a diverse bunch of early-, mid- and late-career artists, producers, administrators, researchers and educators. Many were clearly committed to sustaining long-term opportunities in the sector. Many also noted that a handful of established artists and producers of youth-specific work were carving leadership positions in the wider cultural industry, enabling them to promote and commission innovative new work for the under-25s in more mainstage environments. It's a long-awaited achievement, but the hard work of advocacy and sector development is beginning to pay off. Symposium delegates also contributed to and facilitated over twenty breakout discussions on topics ranging from international touring, urbanism and the built environment, emerging festival models, new Indigenous directions, and the rise of the 'amateur professional', to arts education and how to engage grandparents as arts advocates. Many groups devised action plans during the Symposium to address specific barriers in the sector and all expressed a desire to strengthen the youth-specific sector's connection with the arts and creative industries more broadly.

At the same time, it is fair to say that government support for the sector has become more tangible in this past decade. While maintaining adequate levels of funding will always be cause for concern, there are promising indicators that, at all three tiers of government, there have been positive, long-term initiatives supporting children's creative development. Windmill Theatre in South Australia and Artplay in Melbourne are two examples of high-profile commitments by state and local governments to cater to the needs of children and young people as cultural citizens and artistic collaborators in their own right. Windmill is commissioning innovative new work for young and

family audiences, and is creating productive partnerships with mainstage theatre companies nationally and
internationally; and Artplay engages a wide range of
artists to create and innovate with children and young
people in workshops and events, and enjoys a prime
cultural-precinct position in Melbourne's CBD. The
fact that networks such as Youth Arts Queensland,
Propel Youth Arts, Carclew Youth Arts and Young
People and the Arts Australia are recognized as key
infrastructure partners by their government funding
agencies is also important, as such partnerships enable
long-term security, encourage far-reaching strategy, and
promote responsive sector development.

There's always more to be done. But pity the artist,
producer or bureaucrat who still sees working with or
for young people as just a means to arrive somewhere
else!

What if …

children and young people were more than a tick-a-box priority?

Strong cultural policy plays a pivotal role in posi-
tioning young people effectively in the broader
cultural industry and Australia's civic society.
Prior to the 1990s, young people were most often
represented as 'in deficit' in state and national cultural
policies and strategies. Children and young people
were mostly cast as empty vessels, lacking exposure
to the arts, and needing an education. Involvement

in the arts was promoted as instrumental to their successful development into well-functioning adults. This was a worthy but ultimately limiting aim that failed to acknowledge young people's active participation as creative citizens of the now, not just of the future.

As more inclusive youth-specific arts policies proliferated in the 1990s and early 2000s—major frameworks and strategies were adopted by the Australia Council as well as the Queensland, Western Australian and South Australian state governments— the notion of 'culture' in contemporary cultural policy was expanded. Young people's multiple engagements in everyday creative activity such as skateboarding, computer-gaming, and even extreme sports, were recognized alongside their equally diverse interests in the full spectrum of conventional arts disciplines. Contrary to the claims of conservative observers, this did not mean arts grants went into bungee-jumping and skate competitions, or that money was sucked out of programs for more established artists. Rather, this policy 'movement' saw young people recognized as creators as well as consumers; artists as well as students. Industry induction opportunities, mentoring programs and support for stepping out as emerging artists were some of the resulting strategies—many of which generated employment and active engagement for established artists as workshop facilitators, trainers and mentors. It became almost mandatory for major performing arts organizations to spell out their youth and education programs as a condition for government funding, and niche youth-specific theatre companies came and went, facing all the same survival challenges as small-to-medium organizations across Australia's arts and creative industries.

While these policy developments have been successful to an extent, their flipside, fifteen years later, is that young people have become something of a tick-a-box priority. Once the box has been ticked (yes, this is a 'youth' project), it is difficult to get a clear picture of the quality and effectiveness of broader-based strategies for engaging young people in the arts. For instance, there is a notable lack of publicly available evaluation of government policy initiatives. Granted, it is difficult to assess some outcomes in the youth-specific arts sector that may require costly longitudinal research, but there are very few available reports on the success or otherwise of the implementation of government youth-arts initiatives. Not only does this cloud the sector's understanding of how well (or otherwise) government intervention is working, but it limits our knowledge of inconsistencies and gaps across the general industry. For instance, how commonly is it known that, until recently, very few state, territory or commonwealth government arts agencies even mentioned arts and cultural issues for under-12s and that this age group, despite its flourishing in recent years, rates little attention in policy-making?

Furthermore, as funds are allocated according to the political imperatives of the day, young people are already one step removed from decision-making processes by virtue of the fact that under-18s are ineligible to vote. Gatekeepers therefore abound, whether they be parents, teachers, arts organizations, or benevolent mentors. Importantly, these intermediaries can be effective mediators with vital longer-term perspectives and experience to bear, but the question remains as to how young people are consulted, if at all, and how the results of consultation are reported back to them as follow-up.

There have been frameworks, strategies and policies for young people and the arts that have attempted to be responsive to the cultural economy as well as the contemporary conditions of Australian youth. Yet, by the time policy has moved through slow-moving bureaucracy, strategy development, political approval, and funding allocation, the state of the industry and the generation it targets can have moved on. Could the era of dedicated youth policies therefore be coming to a close? Is the industry (and society) mature enough to accept and support the centrality of children and young people to Australian cultural life, so much so that they are naturally embedded in all industry sector policies and strategies? Sadly, not yet … if at all.

If we were to move on from the tick-a-box mentality, in what other ways could we provide parity among cultural provision for children and young people? A simplistic recasting of how the limited pools of local, state or federal funding get divided up has been flagged in Australia and in other countries. For instance, we've all tried that trick of saying: 'Well, if young people comprise 24% of the population, we demand 24% of available arts funding.' This advocacy strategy can be useful in some contexts, but it's a little naïve if taken to extreme: how valid is it to apportion available investments on age-based criteria in preference to gender, race, socio-economic or art form-based criteria? It's messy, but the demographics argument bears thinking about and could be put to limited strategic use.

But what if we got more big-picture about it? What if government and non-government arts agencies looked to more global policies and conventions to justify and lobby for youth-specific work? The United Nations' Convention on the Rights of the Child, for instance, clearly articulates that children have the right to 'relax and play, and to join in a wide range of cultural, artistic and other recreational activities'.[23] Australia has been a signatory to this Convention since 1991 and, as such, reports regularly on its progress as a nation to the UN Committee on the Rights of the Child.[24] Yet this document is rarely employed by governments or theatre companies as a reference point or advocacy tool to leverage better cultural opportunities for young people.

Artists have always forged new directions in art form development. Funding agencies, particularly those at arms length of government, have a responsibility to foster innovation and make industry-bolstering interventions. Yet, youth-specific arts are slippery policy territory, spanning hybrid and multi-art form styles as well as conventional discipline-based practices. Combined with the instrumentalism of much youth arts work (intersecting as it often does with education, health or welfare), it is often a challenge for youth arts workers to find the right fit for funding programs. This provides both opportunities and pressures: opportunities for greater financial support across a wider range of funding programs, and pressures to justify, define and measure work in a multiplicity of ways removed from the actual practice.

To move beyond children and young people as a tick-a-box priority means to recognize the complexity and multi-disciplinarity of much youth-specific work and acknowledge the many social and economic conditions impacting on young people's creative engagement. For instance, audience development means more than cheap tickets and good relationships with school teachers. First and foremost, it means making really good work that they want to go and see. Then it means connecting with the social networks that young people rely on to communicate with each other. It means awareness of public access and transport options to venues, the timing of performances, the foyer experience, and the follow-up. It means seeking ways to open up touring opportunities for shows both for and by young people. It means identifying how young people develop independence in enacting their cultural lives: how do they buy tickets, when do they buy tickets, and what do they buy tickets with? Who do they attend with and how welcoming are the foyer spaces, the drinks list, and the box-office staff?

If the engagement of children and young people was more than an afterthought, deeper questions as to who the gatekeepers are and how they are engaged would be better considered. For the younger age-groups, strategies now commonplace at Queensland Performing Arts Centre's Out of the Box festival (originally programmed for three-to-eight-year-olds) are relevant here. Producers and volunteers recognize that for many children, their festival experience begins the moment they leave home or school. The bus or train is part of the experience and, once at the site, boxed snack-packs are available as well as interactive and chill-out spaces for inter-performance activity and rest. It's a big day out. Grandparents are valued as attendees, and ushers are trained on appropriate services for parents with prams, hyperactive children, and reluctant first-timers. Lights never fully darken in performance venues, ensuring that younger children don't get frightened, and the audience is reassured that moving about, making verbal responses, and leaving to go to the toilet are all acceptable.

But while many gains have been made in catering to the younger age-groups, older young people have not been so well supported. It is evident that, particularly with major performing arts organizations, youth marketing and participation are conducted through teachers, then parents, and finally young people as students. Many of our Australian colleagues with marketing and publicity responsibilities have said that their main challenge is not how to reach their young audiences, but how to 'get the right teacher on the phone'. Of course, this is vital for marketing education-based programs, and it must be acknowledged that in an age when subscribers and pre-purchasers are waning, school bookings provide welcome economic security. So how are teachers embraced beyond their ticket-purchasing function? How are young people supported in their transition into independent theatre-goers? What understanding do young people have of the various ways in which to buy tickets and access information about shows? Beyond ticking the 'youth' box, how are organizations encouraging and supporting young people to 'buy in' to theatre—not only financially, but culturally—as long-term punters?

And, finally, if young people were more than a tick-a-box priority, the contemporary collapse of the consumer/creator divide would be addressed by creating multiple and diverse entry-points for young people to enable them to extend their theatre experience. In recent years, Queensland Theatre Company (QTC) has been exemplary in this respect, providing a host of opportunities and incentives for young artists and audiences, such as an annual program of three productions targeted for young audiences; a student advisory panel; volunteer intern and secondment positions for theatre students and graduates; mentoring for young emerging artists; opportunities for young people to collaborate with professional artists in school and community-based drama workshops and via QTC's partnerships with youth theatre groups; and scholarships, prizes and support initiatives for young playwrights. These opportunities help contribute to the company's proud statistic that 30% of their total engagement in 2010 was with young people under 30 years of age. This included 15,873 attendances by young people aged between 12 and 30 years at QTC performances, and 18,005 by children under 12. Interestingly, 8,624 students and young people were also engaged as active participants in other QTC activities.[25] While statistics on attendance and participation are just one indicator of the success of these initiatives, we understand from anecdotal evidence that this approach is also contributing to attitudinal change whereby young artists and audiences are feeling valued and central to the QTC community. Could the same be said of all of our country's major performing arts companies?

What if ...

the theatre sector acknowledged the ways in which youth arts practitioners have already cultivated the kinds of well-functioning professional development networks and collaborations that it yearns for?

Youth arts practitioners (those who engage young people in participatory activities), as well as those artists and arts workers creating work for children and young people as audiences, are a well-connected and organized bunch of practitioners. Over the past 30 years, not only has the sector lobbied for and secured support from various tiers and departments of government, but it has also embraced the needs of emerging young artists and the demands of a diverse range of theatre and hybrid performance practices. These developments are evident in the history of peak body Young People and the Arts Australia, which Margaret Leask and Joan Pope established in 1975 as the Youth Performing Arts Association.[26] YPAA has sought to be a strong advocate for youth performing arts and, while its fortunes and its membership have ebbed and flowed over the years, it currently generates supportive national networks and professional development opportunities. Alongside the long-running *Lowdown*,[27] a magazine for youth performing arts published out of the Carclew Youth Arts Centre in Adelaide, it has helped established key infrastructure for the growth of a professional community of artists and arts workers.

In 2008, after 30 years of volunteer and some paid labour, in-kind contributions, small grants and broad membership, YPAA was validated as a national peak body by the Australia Council alongside similar key infrastructure organizations for playwrights, major performing arts companies, venues, other art forms and touring producers. This recognition—and multi-year funding arrangement—in turn provides a national platform that asserts loudly and clearly that this arts practice is relevant and substantive.

YPAA's growth has occurred in concert with that of a number of state-based networking and advocacy bodies, such as Youth Arts Queensland and Propel Arts in Western Australia, as well as significant centres for youth-specific arts established in earlier years, such as Carclew in Adelaide, St Martin's in Melbourne and Shopfront and PACT centres in Sydney. YPAA is also the Australian centre for the Association Internationale du Théâtre pour l'Enfance et la Jeunesse (ASSITEJ: the International Association of Theatre for Children and Young People). ASSITEJ facilitates international networking, touring, and exchange across 80 member countries.

In the past two years, new YPAA initiatives have included the resurrection of a biennial national conference, a new incubator program for companies in growth, and state-based Youth Arts Markets that showcase work created for, with and by young people. YPAA's 'Blueprints' interest groups meet monthly by teleconference, bringing together from across the country groups of practitioners, such as Aboriginal and Torres Strait Islander theatre artists, regional artists, artistic directors, general managers, producers, education officers and workshop coordinators, to discuss common issues and opportunities in a 'real time' community of practice.

Over time, the national sector has developed a suite of festivals including Come Out, Next Wave, Out of the Box, This is Not Art, Sydney Children's Festival and Awesome. The sector has successfully hosted two ASSITEJ World Congress and Festival events on the strength of Australia's reputation for high quality work in the international arena and the advocacy of its hardworking representatives at these times, Tony Mack and before him, Michael FitzGerald. New and relevant professional infrastructure continues to emerge, such as the International Theatre for Children and Young People Researchers' and Critics' Forum, first held in Buenos Aires in 2010. With institutional partners including the International Theatre for Young Audiences Research Network and universities in Norway, Germany, the United States, Turkey and Korea, this inaugural international forum featured Australian practitioners Claudia Chidiac and Finegan Kruckemeyer, presenting on topics such as 'The manipulation of innocence on Australian stages' and 'The taboo of sadness'.

The sector is getting pretty good at building links and partnerships with the wider theatre industry. In 2000, Zeal Theatre was contracted by Sydney Theatre Company to present their two-hander, *The Stones*, as part of STC's education program. By 2005, Zeal company members Tom Lycos and Stefo Nantsou were also conducting workshops and other activities in the STC's annual youth and education programs. Three education program commissions were followed by the opportunity to work on a mainstage performance as well as more integrated involvement in the company's program overall. In 2009, Zeal became an associate company of STC and co-produced with the mainstage program, *Burnt*, an original play based on the real-life stories of regional Australians suffering prolonged drought. Originally a schools' touring company, Zeal offered STC their expertise in creating work for young audiences and in connecting with young people through plays that spoke directly to their experience. STC offered Zeal not only working space, but also administrative and production support, allowing the small two-person outfit to concentrate on creating new work and growing a greater profile. The partnership was clearly a win-win situation: STC was able to co-produce relevant theatre for young audiences across its education and mainstage programs, and Zeal was able to continue its signature style of work and commitment to young people. As Nantsou commented of the situation, 'We managed to help each other.'[28]

In 2008, the new Theatre Network Victoria (TNV) was established, taking responsibility for hosting the previously discussed inaugural Australian Theatre

Forum in 2009. It is not surprising that six of the nine founding companies of the network had a youth focus and five of the 11 representatives on the current steering committee work specifically with young people and emerging artists. Theatre practitioners working in the youth-specific sector understand the value of regional, national and international networks. The youth-specific arts sector provides a model framework for deepening critical conversations, strengthening national and international networks, and fostering productive partnerships. Rather than being perceived as having limited knowledge or little contribution to make to the wider theatre industry, practitioners working with young people are already sharing and leading the industry in matters of national concern. They just haven't shouted about it yet.

What if ...

the Australian theatre industry recognized that young artists and the leading edge of international and Australian youth-specific performance have a lot to offer adult audiences and can signal vital new trends?

Theatre by, for and with young people is forging new directions in form and is building new audiences. In particular, the opportunities that participatory youth theatre provides to collectively explore form and content have given rise to extraordinary new works that signal the cutting edge of contemporary performance practice. Belgian theatre company Ontroerend Goed, for example, recently toured with a group of young people aged 14 to 18, performing their devised work *Once And For All We're Gonna Tell You Who We Are So Shut Up And Listen*. Keynote speaker at the YPAA symposium, director Alexander Devriendt described his approach to developing the work as 12 months of 'letting young people simply be themselves on stage'. This free-range approach culminated in a selection of performative gests, scaffolded into a loose dramatic structure that provided the backbone to a theatre event that was a fresh and different experience every time on stage. In *Once And For All*, there is little pretence or self-conscious characterization on the part of the young performers. They douse each other in paint, muck around making plastic-cup castles, trade mock blows and allegiances and, in quite a profound way, simply share time on stage. It is a disarmingly open piece and during its two years of international touring its live honesty moved adult and young audiences alike. The flipside of its immediacy, however, was its limited shelf-life: the piece was not replicable with a replacement cast and yet, as the original players grew older and began to experience the world differently, the show was no longer authentically theirs to share. As one of the YPAA delegates expressed it, in response to Devriendt's work, 'No one in Australia lets young people do shit like this, it's so honest and real, we are so afraid.'[29]

Similarly, Mammalian Diving Reflex, a Canadian theatre company directed by Darren O'Donnell, has evolved a 'social acupuncture' wing that has moved away from conventional theatre performance to the creation of conceptual performances with young people and others in public settings. They have produced the abovementioned *Haircuts by Children* as well as *Eat the Streets*, whereby children aged ten to 12 years are engaged as restaurant critics, inviting the audience/community to share meals with them as they rate the experience. Similarly, the company's *Children's Choice Awards* have become a popular feature of performing arts festivals internationally, as juries of local young people review the work they see, engage in some playful paparazzi-style interactions with artists, and host an awards ceremony. These works are revelatory and, for some audiences, unsettling, as the dramatic effect emerges from the very real tension of having young people in positions of power usually entrusted to those with sanctioned expertise. Yet it is in many ways a generous kind of aesthetic activism: young performers invite their audience-members in on the act (by having their hair cut, sharing a meal, engaging in critical conversation). By way of 'social acupuncture'—the puncturing of social mores—Mammalian's work is part art-installation, part real-time verbatim theatre.

Melbourne's Polyglot Puppet Theatre also draws on an art-installation aesthetic in *We Built This City*, which continues to tour internationally. In this project, conceptualized by artistic drector Sue Giles, a large play-space comprising hundreds of cardboard boxes is created for children in a major public space. Aided by jaunty adult co-artists in requisite hard hats and overalls, the children are required to design and re-design their city, thereby offering creative insight into the attributes of their current and dream built environments. Apart from the very real fun of knocking it all down if it's not quite right, *We Built This City*, like Mammalian's work, hosts a take-over of public space that is both performative and critically reflexive.

These artists know all too well the power of having young people present theatrical work back to adult audiences. In a period of such immense generational change, performance becomes a potent vehicle for civic real-time interactions between adults and young people. Where the internet may have collapsed the divide between consumer and creator, this kind of work displays a related reworking of the implied contract between performer and audience. Its rawness can be disarming and, while it will never take the place of more traditional theatre forms, it gives a clue to the impact of the new creative economy on young people's necessary search for and expression of authenticity and identity.

In the late 1990s, twelve young women were mentored and supported by leading theatre practitioners Maryanne Lynch and Louise Gough to create short one-woman shows in a project called *Stampede*, co-presented by Backbone Youth Arts and Playlab in Queensland. The work was showcased at a nightclub in Fortitude Valley called The Zoo, as part of Two High, which at that time was a Young Women's Arts Festival. The Zoo was the site for much youth-arts activity around this time and was a grungy alternative to conventional contemporary theatre spaces, to which young and emerging artists had very little access. By 2010, Two High had not only grown to include young men, but was run at the Brisbane Powerhouse, a 'real' live-arts venue. The festival engages a far greater number of participants and employs roughly 15 young and emerging artists as coordinators.

Opportunities like those offered by Two High have multiplied in Australia over the past 15 years. Initiatives like these put young artists in a context: providing training, mentoring and other personal connections to professional artists and arts workers in the industry. This in turn creates something like a quality assurance process: young artists get honest feedback from their mentors and develop industry networks about their work. Yet even with this growing support, for many younger practitioners conventional live theatre is simply an unaffordable art form. As a young woman visiting the YPAA office commented recently, 'It would cost me about $40,000 to put on a theatre show, like, properly....What young person can afford that?'

Young emerging theatre artists have had to become savvy to work their way around obstacles to their participation in the theatre industry. They do so either by merging with broader youth-arts organizations, as young women in the Stampede project did, getting a gig with a formal mentoring program like the Australia Council's Jump, or else they simply do what artists from a range of art form areas have been doing for centuries—DIY.

The Do-It-Yourself culture is strong in Australia among a range of age-groups, although it has become even more so with young people in our current climate-changing, social-networking culture. Within contemporary performance practice, DIY takes an interesting form. No longer a punk gig held in someone's backyard, it might be a soap opera experienced via personal ipods at designated times and places in the city. DIY performance features young artists bypassing theatre rental and hefty production costs by innovating with 'non-venue' performance events. The trend is particularly evident in festivals. Andrew Dickson and Lyn Gardner observed of the 2010 Edinburgh Festival Fringe that 'performers are choosing stranger settings than ever', utilizing the drama of the street and environment itself.[30] By way of example, they discuss Invisible Dot's tele-drama, performed over the phone in iconic red UK phone-booths; Laura Muggridge's performance in a campervan; a new work presented in a video rental store; and the work of Australian company En Route. En Route artists Suzanne Kerston, Clair Korobarz, Paul Moir and Julian Ricket invite audience-members to use their personal ipods and mobile phones to navigate their way around back streets and interesting spaces in inner-urban landscapes. In these environments, the audience-member is instructed to watch various performers whom they might not otherwise notice, developing a multi-site evolving work.

This is not to suggest that all street-based performances are born of economic necessity. Take Back to Back's outstanding *small metal objects* which would have required a significant budget for the use of electronic equipment and audience seating in its many 'venues'. But, for our sample of young artists, it can be the case of necessity being the proverbial mother of invention.

Digital technologies underpinning these kinds of DIY works are being further explored in increasingly sophisticated ways by youth-specific companies and young artists. For instance, in *Short Message Service*, a work created by Leah Shelton and Lachlan Tetlow-Stuart for the 2010 Next Wave Festival, audience members are invited to text the actors from their mobile phones, telling them what to do. Two 'operators' decipher the messages and relay them to the actors verbally through headphones and to audience members via live projection on stage. Each night the narrative evolves differently, blurring conventional boundaries for audiences, and frequently unsettling them. For instance, during one performance, the screened text instructed the actors to take off their tops and leave the theatre. The actors declined. Was this their choice or had the 'operators' mediated the texts received and modified their instructions? Who was really shaping the work? What was an audience member to do, when offended by the instructions of others? Part game, part experiment, *Short Message Service* uses mobile-phone technology to investigate what happens when a group of strangers seemingly exert control over a couple of volunteers.

Similarly, Adelaide's Border Project engages digital technologies to blur the relationship between audience and performer in a DIY way. Artistic Director Sam Haren indicated that the six company members wanted 'a sophisticated way for the audience to input and make things happen during the work'. Accordingly, with support from the Inter-Arts Office of the Australia Council, a small hand-held device was developed for the audience to use during performances, bringing the 'choose your own adventure novel' concept to the theatre. While it has proved popular with the company's target audience of non-theatregoers and young people, it has placed additional pressure on the creative team, as they devised approximately 250 scenes in preparation for their 2008 show, *Trouble on Planet Earth*.[31] By the end of the season there were still some ten scenes that the audience had never chosen to see.

In the international arena, Ontroerend Goed's latest work, *Teenage Riot*, evolved from director Devriendt's fascination with the idea that YouTube, unlike television or cinema, makes little distinction between fact and fiction. Following *Once And For All...*, *Teenage Riot* again features young people 'just being themselves', but in an enclosed room on stage. They are only visible to the audience via what we assume is a live-feed video projection on screen. It has a rather more curated DIY feel than earlier works mentioned, but one that similarly challenges the conventional artist and audience pact and offers new experiences each time it is performed. While the question of what is real and what is not has consumed artists for centuries, it is providing fodder for new explorations of representation and identity by young artists both skilled and subversive in their use of digital media and theatrical conventions.

In another area of youth-specific work, Australian artists are exploring what has been described as the 'last frontier of audience development': theatre for under-three-year-olds. Last year saw the completion of two Australia Council Fellowships, by Sally

Chance and Tony Mack, exploring new practice in movement-based performance and theatre with babies and preverbal children. To consider the impact of theatrical experience on this age-group is to get to the very core of theatre's value as a communicative art form. Again, it disturbs conventional views on the audience-artist relationship and the value of script, narrative and character; but it also throws into relief the ways in which theatre for broader audiences critically employ space and intimacy in performance. Long creative-development time underscored by interaction with target audiences and extensive research provides a model for good practice in any sector of the theatre industry: in the case of Chance's work in particular, it ensures a deepening of, and international profile for, new Australian work of this type.

A further trend in interactive theatre for and by young people is performance for small audiences. Recent works include the abovementioned project by En Route, as well as Melbourne-based Tipsy Teacup Production's *A Little Piece*, which invites up to six members of the audience at a time to experience a show in a small cube. The performance has a child-friendly scale and is innovative in its use of multiple theatrical forms, including puppetry, storytelling and interactive visual artworks. It still offers a 'wow' factor for children, while being a special event shared with just a few others at a time. Yet, small-audience shows, regardless of their growing popularity with children and young people as audiences and artists, complicate matters for venues and producers trying to score big box office. Examples of similar work globally suggest that festivals provide the best possible conditions for the scheduling of this kind of work so that producers can reap regular ticket prices for the opportunity to experience a number of small-audience works on the one ticket. And while theatre for small audiences might seem akin to the ten-minute Short and Sweet theatre movement, it is not. Small-audience theatre is about a different kind of personalization of performance that, similar to the challenge of producing theatre for babies, gets to the heart of why and how live art matters in the first place. Whether these artists seek a genuine connection with audiences (as in the case of Tipsy Teacup), or whether they attempt to be ironic about their aim (as in Ontroerend Goed's production), performances with this level of intimacy speak to the social condition of children and young people. They play on the borderlands of fear and trust, revealing much about contemporary Australian social attitudes and connections with the young.

The part of our theatre industry that is driven by box office has yet to see the value in these theatre and performance trends. But we believe that they offer important insights into the expectations and interest of young (and other) audience members and artists now so used to 'culture on demand'. With small-audience theatre and the kinds of performance installation and interactivity we've discussed, the audience feels more catered for: this experience is individual, personal and unique. With 'non-venue' and more interactive works, the experience changes every time. For some, working with these forms not only provides a way to overcome the obstacles they experience in trying to create new work, it delivers the kind of intimate and connected performance experience that new audiences crave. Much of this work might reference styles, experiments, and theories across theatre's history, but the ability to create a live experience that is specific both to the audience and the environment it encounters is relevant and worth our attention. As a young person says in *Once And For All*, 'Everything might have been done before. But not by me. And not now.'

What if ...

young punters camped out to get their tickets to the next state-theatre show, as they might for the next Big Day Out?

N ot likely.
But let's set our sights on the marketing game and again fantasize 'what if ...'.

We've tried here to avoid over-simplistic generationalist distinctions. We've intentionally created slippage between the terms 'children' and 'young people', although we're acutely aware of the differences between age-groups. But at some point we need to acknowledge how young people are framed in Australia's popular imaginary. So, for the purposes of this essay, we acknowledge that the young cohort we are referring to here is commonly known as 'Gen Y'; and their impact on Australia's cultural and creative industries is only now beginning to take shape.

In the 1990s, Mark Davis's *Gangland: Cultural Elites and the New Generationalism* became a much-cited book about the Baby Boomers' stranglehold on Australia's cultural leadership and the dire implications for their continued cultural gatekeeping, particularly for the then-emerging Gen X. While aspects of Davis's argument still ring true—and he makes a cogent argument for abandoning generationalist discourse in the first place—little attention has yet been paid to the implications and influence of Gen Y on the nation's cultural landscape. This may be due to the fact that the internet has become a far more accessible and relevant tool for Gen Y content-creators and visionaries (why bother trying to put your points or your art across in mainstream avenues?) and partly because they're still an unknown to the generations preceding them.

So what can we glean about the Gen Y phenomenon and what value does this knowledge have for the fostering of new artists and audiences in the theatre industry? Nearly 4.5 million Australians born between 1982 and 2000 are categorized as Gen Ys. Sometimes referred to as the first generation of 'digital natives', these are the cohort of young people growing up with advanced computer technology as the norm and with the internet as an everyday part of their lives (unless they experience significant social and economic disadvantage or live in a regional or remote area). Characteristics commonly projected on Gen Y include:

- They're plugged in
- TV isn't king
- They don't care about ads; they care what their friends think

- Work isn't their whole world
- They're socially conscious.[32]

While this appears to us a fairly cursory list of traits, it is important to recognize that the Gen Y category comprises around 28 per cent of the population and, while Gen Xs and Ys continue to give birth to their 'Generation Z' children (!), the Gen Y cohort will continue to be the focus for generating ticket sales, new work, and transitional leadership of the theatre industry for some years to come.

So how to connect with this age-group without homogenizing their interests or assuming that they share mass generational values and tastes? The big music festivals, like the national travelling Big Day Out, know how to, but they have the advantage of multiple bands for multiple tastes, the thrill of large party-like crowds, and the triple bottom-line of drinking, dancing and (maybe) drugs. But let's consider another, less predominantly youth-focused, industry—travel.

The travel industry, although it caters to intergenerational consumers, has got the gist of how young people want to be participants, and not simply passive consumers. Take the classic tourist-industry campaigns for tropical island holidays. Look in any *Australian Weekend Magazine* and you'll find ads for island vistas offering tranquil, rejuvenating, spa-indulged experiences. As a potential consumer, you are coaxed to *put yourself in the picture*. Gen Ys, on the other hand, want to *make the picture*. To see what this means, look at the homepage www.lonelyplanet.com or follow the 'explore the world' link on www.statravel.com.au. This is not about characterizing a generation by their interests in adventure travel and backpacking. It is an acknowledgment of the changed social context in which young people, as opposed to their older siblings and parents, operate. Young people identified as Gen Y want to be able to share whatever they encounter and integrate their experience into the networks they create, whether they are planning to spend a gap year volunteering in Sri Lanka, a five-night football-team breakup in Bali, or a weekend in Sydney. Savvy travel agencies, such as STA Travel, know that they will cultivate loyalty with Gen Y not solely by selling cheap tickets (which is still critical), but by encouraging young people to build a range of experiences and help enable them to document and critique those experiences with and for others.

The travel industry has also capitalized on the fact that the best marketing is by word-of-mouth, which is all the more potent with Facebook, Twitter and MySpace. Google has taken this further with its 'Favorite Places' platform. Travel and other businesses are encouraged to display a Google code at their premises so that when a photograph of the place is taken, it can be automatically deciphered and linked to Google maps and further online information. For some, this may seem like hyper-consumerism gone crazy, but for young people (and others), it is a means of value-adding the experience they share with others as they click on to flickr and tubmlr to document their experiences and share them with the world.

It's not such a big leap to see how these same principles and strategies are relevant to the theatre industry. Of course, many theatre companies already utilize Facebook and Twitter for marketing purposes. But, for a more expansive vision that encompasses not just marketing but cultural access, what if companies enabled and encouraged young people to build a range of experiences and relationships with their theatre 'products'? Consider QTC's model of a multiple entry-point approach, which is contributing to a very healthy 30% benchmark of young audiences and participants. If young artists and those who work with young people were genuinely valued for their expertise in identifying and cultivating these entry points (and utilizing the everyday digital media young people use to help do so), really productive collaborations between mainstage and youth-specific sectors could result in positive crossover effect to generate relevant programming and attract new audiences.

Generation X and the Baby Boomers who preceded them have embraced digital media, social networking and technology, but arguably they do old things with new technologies. By contrast, Gen Y does new things with new technologies. So, rather than sticking with conventional strategies that try to sell a theatre show by making it look like a cool thing to see, companies would be well advised to devise more multidimensional strategies around engagement and interactivity (even for the David Williamsons on the program). Some festivals, such as Out of the Box, Brisbane Festival and the recent Junction 2010 in Tasmania, have integrated blogging projects into their programs. This can be risky business: most bloggers do not carry the responsibility of making a living from their comment and therefore sometimes fail to take due care. But, as Wikipedia demonstrates, participants collectively tend to correct, and blogs can be great platforms for expressing diversity of opinion and taste. Ultimately, if the quality of the performance experience is good enough, effective online promotion will follow.

As for touring, Ben Cameron shares a bold and democratic strategy devised by Misnomer Dance Theatre in the US to engage new audiences and facilitate touring to regional areas. Misnomer streamed a dance work on the internet and invited people to watch it online for free. The company then identified the regions where the largest groups of online viewers were located and scheduled tours to the closest towns. This is an example of using new technology in new ways—not only to introduce their work to a broader audience, but to identify places where new audiences could be developed, and help the chances of healthy ticket sales.

Australian organizations are taking note. The current Arts Queensland touring strategy, *Coming to a Place near You*, aims to give audiences a greater say in what tours to their regions.[33] It features research campaigns that engage communities in identifying their arts-touring preferences and invites the Queensland public to evaluate their arts-touring experiences on a dedicated blog. The strategy democratises decision-making to a certain extent by establishing a more direct relationship with the audience. When people are welcomed into a process and invited to collaborate in meaningful ways, they take ownership of the outcomes: they promote the touring product and share it with friends, colleagues, and family members.

Contemporary-music groups have employed this strategy for some time and there is a wealth of online examples of fans and punters who are taking the lead in determining where bands tour.

In the meantime, while online ticketing may have taken the fun out of camping overnight for prized tickets to big-name events, what if Gen Y were as eager as that—and independently so—to get their theatre tickets as soon as they went on sale?

There is a variety of potential 'sharing' initiatives that can be built into the theatre experience for young audience members in order to help achieve long-term interest and effect. For instance, if a composer or musical director has been engaged in the development of a show, could the music be purchased from itunes after the show? Or perhaps audience members could receive a free music download with their ticket purchase? Many theatre companies create education packs for teachers but, for the independent young theatregoer, what about take-home packs with references to websites where they can download music or video clips from the performance to upload on Facebook and show to friends? What about artists' blogs, set and costume drawings, even behind-the-scenes bloopers? What if company-commissioned photographers roamed the foyer to capture young audience members' energy and style and posted images directly to their phones or the web, allowing young people to then curate their own galleries of the experience to share with wider networks?

If some of these ideas seem too cutesy for the 'serious stuff of theatre', what about sharing knowledge with young people in one-off interactive or open rehearsals, which in turn enable young people to act as sounding boards and artistic advisors? This audience-centred process was successfully implemented and documented by Arena Theatre's *Play Dirty*, a show directed by Rose Myer that featured live motocross and performed in a shed on Melbourne's docklands. It was also employed by Susan Richer in her many commissions during her term as director of Out of the Box. In Richer's and Myer's work, young people were engaged in the earliest stages of concept development and, in the case of *Play Dirty*, students were encouraged to chart the progress of the play, read about professional motocross riders, and watch work-in-progress showings, while at the same time giving input and feedback on the creative process. These multiple interactions with young people leading up to the performance of *Play Dirty* at the 2002 Melbourne International Arts Festival were a significant factor in attracting 5000 people to see the show. This approach provides an example of integrated engagement and audience development, as opposed to cursory tick-a-box consultation.

Polyglot also demonstrates good practice in ensuring young people who act as advisors do so in ways that are appropriate to their age, ability, and comfort-zone. Director Sue Giles uses multiple means for youth inter-action, including drawing and drama games alongside conventional chats around a table. Practitioners who work with young people know it's no good just asking young people what they think or dropping them into board meetings. If due care and attention are not paid to their own ways of communicating, their involvement will only ever be token.

Furthermore, there are myriad 'small step' strategies that can be taken. Ushers, ticketing agents and security guards could be urged to get to know this cohort a little better and be encouraged to communicate with them and accept and welcome them into the theatre experience, rather than regarding them as a potential disruption.

In fostering a more robust ecology of Australian theatre, professional and established artists could be offered incentives to attend youth theatre regularly, to show support, gain a greater understanding of the kind of work young people are producing, and to talk with participants after the shows about their artistic choices. What if there was an annual national patron-, ambassador- or mentor-award to ensure that this happened and it became a coveted badge of honour for established artists? While current mentor programs like Jump are fostering the development of individual emerging artists, other high-profile incentives for established artists to engage with the youth-specific sector would also promote a greater understanding and profile for youth-specific work more generally. Children's and young people's artistry is integral to the industry's development and long-term sustainability. It needs to be the business of all practitioners, and not simply those dedicated few who commit to work professionally with the under-25s.

What if mainstage and major performing-arts organizations brought young people in on the act of translating and/or producing performances or performance excerpts in different languages in various suburbs, as a way of welcoming diverse families and communities into theatre experiences? Many young people already translate for older family members in everyday settings. What an opportunity this would offer to enjoy a theatre experience together. And so many larger theatre companies concentrate on their main CBD stage and then 'the regions'; but what about what's in between—the outer suburbs? What if more theatre experiences were multi-dimensional, encouraging, for instance, new language knowledge as Big hART recently did with *Ngapartji Ngapartji*? What if the theatre industry recognized the multicultural leadership already present in the industry, to the extent that, when engaging young people from culturally diverse communities, they are not just seen as another tick-a-box of 'others'? What if there was an effort to engage in genuine connection with young people of diverse cultures, so that they felt safe in the knowledge that their involvement was going to be worthwhile, respected and culturally-appropriate within their communities—much like the approach of Contact Inc or Urban Theatre Projects?

Returning to the question of intermediaries, what if young people beyond the age of 13 were enabled and encouraged to become independent theatre-audience members and participants? This is a difficult age-group to engage, regardless of context, and for many producers it has become too hard, as we've already indicated. There is currently a dearth of work out there for the post-13s and, for the health of the national theatre industry, there's a lot riding on keeping them engaged and interested into adulthood. Bred on a gatekeeper model of participation, however, young people too often sever the link with theatre when it comes time to drop drama class, leave school or get a job. Indeed, it still comes as a shock to hear of school career-counsellors advising academically strong humanities students to 'use their smarts' and strive for tertiary entrance into 'prestige courses' such as law, before considering arts, let alone creative arts. This approach serves to devalue not only a career in the arts, but the arts more generally. And while it is true that creative-arts graduates' earnings are notoriously low compared to others, on what other indicators of graduate satisfaction apart from earnings are counsellors basing their advice? Is anyone even providing such indicators? And who's taking responsibility for unpacking the unhelpful obsession with celebrity that is impeding students' understanding and expectation of what a career in the performing arts can entail?

In conclusion, what if ...

quite simply, young people were brought in on the act of transforming Australian theatre?

In earlier years, the young people's theatre sector was fairly simply defined by its three categories of work: theatre-in-education, theatre for young people, and youth theatre. For years these categories have determined the way in which youth-specific work has been funded, valued, analysed and eventually made. Yet, the practices and issues of this sector are far more broad, complicated, critically engaging and interdependent with those of the 'main' Australian theatre industry than that. So it's time that this straitjacket was flung off and that the theatre industry fostered youth engagement as an integrated and integral process, rather than an add-on concern.

Practitioners making performance for, by and with young people in Australia right now are facing the same kinds of issues that all Australian theatre-practitioners are facing: the challenge of more accessible creative outlets, touring opportunities, erosion of audiences, and lack of money and jobs. Yet those in the youth sector of the industry have had to develop myriad approaches to managing constant change—due in no small part to the need to be alert to the chameleon tastes, interests and obsessions of children, post-13s, and young adults. The youth sector has learnt that the most effective of these approaches place young people at the centre of meaningful consultation and two-way participation. Recent outstanding internationally awarded work, like Slingsby's *The Magical Life of Cheeseboy* and Real TV's *Hoods*, show that this need not compromise artistic vision, independence and quality professional product capable of attracting wider-ranging audiences. Nor does it mean overhauling mainstage programming, as successful partnerships between Sydney Theatre Company and Zeal Theatre, and Sydney Opera House and many small-to-medium companies demonstrate. Nor does it let young participants get away with sloppy dramaturgy or production values when they devise their own work, as the quality of recent Riverland Youth Theatre and Carriageworks performances demonstrates. Now, as we enter a new world order of participatory creativity, there's a lot that our 'older' culture industries can take from the youth sector's approach. As youth-theatre practitioners and wise grandparents have known for some time, there's a lot to learn from children and young people. Sharing our cultural authority has real rewards.

We all have a responsibility to put some of the *community* back into our national theatre industry. For instance, why is rounding up youth audiences mostly left to education and outreach officers and teachers? If a teenager wants to go to the movies, a concert, or a music festival, they most definitely have the networks, advanced information-retrieval skills, and the street smarts to work out how to secure funds, book tickets, liaise with friends, organize transport, reassure parents, decide on what to wear, and have a brilliant time. Why don't they do this for theatre? Could it be that our theatres are simply not that accessible—physically or culturally? Marketing rarely reaches young people directly, ticketing mechanisms are adhoc according to the level of administrative infrastructure enjoyed by the company (and what if you don't have a credit card?), venues are often physically unwelcoming and even simple things like adequate signage—which means a great deal to young people—is often lacking. There's a hidden culture to attending some theatres and if young people have mostly experienced getting to theatre by stepping off a school bus, they'll be unlikely to know for sure if they can access or be welcomed to the place when on their own or with their friends.

We strongly advocate—and we work in—school-based arts education and theatre that support school curricula, but what further efforts can the industry make to listen to, collaborate with, and learn from children and young people, acknowledging them as the creative citizens and agents that they are?

When it comes to addressing children's and young people's engagement in theatre, we echo Susan Richer's refusal to be satisfied with the national by-line 'it's all good'. Surely there are plenty of young artists doing great edgy work all by themselves, providing the compost of Australian theatre with independent shows and fresh new faces? ... Isn't arts education already at the starting gate of the next round of national curricula development? ... Don't our major arts orgs already deliver mandatory education and youth access programs? ... Yes, yes and sometimes. But we suggest that these features alone may be less than good enough in an industry that's still reeling from the realization of just how 'live' and immediate creative interaction has become outside the theatre stalls. We may be doing moderately OK, helping to put young people in the picture, but are we creating opportunities for them to *make* the picture?

There's much more we can do to cultivate an interactive and dynamic theatre ecology in this country. We can start by recognizing the gains and increasing value of a vibrant youth-specific sector—in and beyond capital city Australia. In the face of such rapid and unsettling culture-change, young people are a much greater resource and driver for positive and responsive industry-change than most of us realize.

Endnotes

1 See Australia Council, *Data on Artists' Employment and Professional Practice in Australia October 2009*, Senate Standing Committee on Environment, Communications and the Arts (February 2010) as discussed by Christopher Madden, 'Australia's Creative Revolution', at http://artspolicies. org/2010/07/05/australias-creative-revolution (5 July 2010) (accessed 10 August 2010).

2 Positive Solutions, *Review of Theatre for Young People in Australia* (Sydney: Australia Council for the Arts, 2003).

3 See website and updates for this project at http:// theatrespace.org.au (accessed 4 August 2010).

4 As pointed out by Ben Cameron, Program Director, Arts of the Doris Duke Charitable Foundation, in his keynote speech at the 2009 Australia Council Arts Marketing Summit. Entitled 'On the Brink of a New Chapter: Arts in the Twenty-First Century', the speech is available at http://www.australi-acouncil.gov.au/__data/assets/pdf_file/0005/59864/ Ben_Cameron_Speech_final_speech.pdf (accessed 1 August 2010).

5 See Marcus Westbury, 'Has the Australia Council had its Day?', *Age*, online, 26 July 2010, at http:// www.theage.com.au/entertainment/art-and-design/ has-the-australia-council-had-its-day-20100725- 10qgt.html (accessed 1 August 2010), extracted

from an article he wrote with Ben Eltham, 'Cultural Policy in Australia', in *More Than Luck: Ideas Australia Needs Now*, ed. by M. Davis and M. Lyons, Centre for Policy Development Limited. Available at http://morethanluck.cpd.org.au/sharing-the-luck/cultural-policy-in-australia/ (accessed 25 August 2010). The *Age* followed Westbury's article the next day with an extract from an essay by Richard Mills, Director of the West Australian Opera, entitled 'Let us Defend our Heritage Arts', *Age*, 27 July 2010. A flurry of blogs and newspaper articles followed in response, including Ben Eltham's 'The Heritage Wars Heat Up' on *A Cultural Policy Blog*, http://culturalpolicyreform.wordpress.com/2010/08/06/the-heritage-wars-heat-up/, 6 August 2010 (accessed 10 October 2010) and another by Christopher Madden, 'In Defence of the Australia Council', 5 August 2010, http://artspolicies.org/ (accessed 10 October 2010).

6   'How Cognitive Surplus will Change the World', TED Talks, at http://www.ted.com/talks/clay_shirky_how_cognitive_surplus_will_change_the_world.html (accessed 13 October 2010).

7   See http://www.ushahidi.com/ (accessed 13 October 2010).

8   'Small change: Why the Revolution will not be Tweeted', *New Yorker*, 4 October 2010, pp. 42–9.

9   'On the Brink of a New Chapter'. For details, see note 4 above.

10   According to ACNeilsen research. For a summary of their Australian statistics, see 'Australia Getting More Social Online as Facebook Leads and Twitter Grows', 23 March 2010, at http://blog.nielsen.com/nielsenwire/global/australia-getting-more-social-online-as-facebook-leads-and-twitter-grows/ (accessed 10 August 2010).

11   See Australian Bureau of Statistics' article, 'Internet Access at Home', Australian Social Trends 2008, at http://www.abs.gov.au/AUSSTATS/abs@.nsf/Lookup/4102.0Chapter10002008 (accessed 2 October 2010).

12   See Australian Bureau of Statistics article, 'Internet Use and Mobile Phones', Children's Participation in Cultural and Leisure Activities, Australia, April 2009, at http://www.abs.gov.au/ausstats/abs@.nsf/Products/4901.0~Apr+2009~Main+Features~Internet+use+and+mobile+phones?OpenDocument (accessed 2 October 2010).

13   See ABS, 'Cultural Venues and Events: Children's Participation in Cultural and Leisure Activities', Australia, April 2009, at http://www.abs.gov.au/ausstats/abs@.nsf/Latestproducts/4901.0Main%20Features6Apr%202009?opendocument&tabname=Summary&prodno=4901.0&issue=Apr%202009&num=&view (accessed 2 October 2010).

14   (Sydney: Australia Council, 2010), p. 34.

15   In the case of Come Out, the festival's board was motivated by a report by the Government of South Australia's Thinker in Residence, early childhood development expert Dr J. Fraser Mustard, on the importance of the first three years of life. Therefore, it sought to expand programming at the babies' end (telephone conversation with Andy Packer, October 2010). The Awesome team benchmarked their festival with eight other international festivals and identified a growing trend in audience development for the under-13s, including the development of high quality new works for the pre-teenage group. Re-focusing Awesome was a priority and this shift enabled their resources to be utilized for the

best outcomes (telephone interview with Jenny Simpson, 2 November 2010).

16 Marcus Westbury, 'What's so Special about Opera', Festival of Dangerous Ideas, 3 October 2010. See the transcript at http://www.marcuswestbury. net/2010/10/06/whats-so-special-about-opera-my-festival-of-dangerous-ideas (accessed 13 October 2010).

17 David Throsby and Anita Zednik, *Do You Really Expect to Get Paid?: An Economic Study of Professional Artists in Australia* (Sydney: Australia Council, 2010); Stuart Cunningham and others, *What's Your Other Job?: A Census Analysis of Arts Employment in Australia* (Sydney: Australia Council, 2010).

18 'Cultural Policy in Australia'. For details, see note 5 above.

19 'On the Brink of a New Chapter'. For details, see note 4 above.

20 See 'A Quiet Kind of Magic: Young People's Performance in Australia', in *Australian Theatre in the 2000s*, ed. by Richard Fotheringham (Amsterdam: Rodopi Press, forthcoming).

21 *More than Bums on Seats: Australian Participation in the Arts. Research summary*.

22 For a more detailed examination, see John O'Toole and Penny Bundy, 'Kites and Magpies: TIE in Australia', in *Learning through Theatre: New Perspectives on Theatre in Education*, ed. by Tony Jackson (London: Routledge, 1993), pp. 133–49.

23 Article 31 of Convention of the Rights of the Child, Office of the United Nations High Commissioner for Human Rights (entry into force 2 September 1990), at http://www2.ohchr.org/english/law/crc. htm#art31 (accessed 2 August 2010).

24 See 'What's up, Croc? Australia's Implementation of the Convention on the Rights of the Child' , at http://www.ncylc.org.au/croc/allaboutcroc1.html (accessed 3 August 2010).

25 Statistics on youth engagement in QTC performances and programs in 2010, as at 16 November 2010, kindly supplied by Joseph Mitchell, Resident Director, QTC.

26 For further information on the establishment of YPAA, see Margaret Leask, 'Acknowledging the Past: Youth Performing Arts in the 1970s', *Australasian Drama Studies* 47 (2005), pp. 14–25.

27 In 2009, *Lowdown* became a fully online journal. See http://www.lowdown.net.au.

28 Personal interview with Stefo Nantsou, 15 October 2010.

29 Candy Bowers in conversation with Lenine Bourke, Brisbane, 10 June 2009.

30 'The Edinburgh Festival's Oddest Theatre Locations', *Guardian*, 9 August 2010, at http://www.guardian.co.uk/culture/video/2010/aug/09/edinburgh-festival-theatre (accessed 10 August 2010).

31 Personal interview with Sam Haren, 3 December 2009.

32 Peter Sheahan, *Generation Y: Thriving and Surviving with Generation Y at Work* (Melbourne: Hardie Grant, 2006).

33 See Queensland Government, 'Arts Queensland Touring Strategy', at http://www.arts.qld.gov.au/policy/tourstrategy.html (accessed 25 August 2010).

Readers' Forum

Response to Erin Brannigan's *Moving Across Disciplines: Dance in the 21st Century*, (Platform Papers 25)

Amanda Card lectures in the Department of Performance Studies, University of Sydney. Her areas of research include dance and performance histories, cross-cultural and hybrid performance, and theories of embodiment. She is the author of Platform Papers 8, *Body for Hire? The State of Dance in Australia*.

Erin Brannigan's ability to draw out and draw upon the articulate reflections of contemporary performance makers has been regularly displayed in her contributions to the contemporary arts magazine *RealTime*. They are again on display in her Currency House Platform Paper, No.25, where she engages in eloquent reflections that could be identified as the work of a good journalist. But her process is also akin to the expertise of an anthropologist: a researcher who engages in 'field work' and takes the time to ask of her informants 'What do you think you're doing?' For me, this is what makes her essay a most exciting, stimulating and useful contribution to the discussion of local dance practice. Particularly in the sections on 'Interdisciplinary continuity' and 'Interdisciplinary dance in Australia', Erin deftly frames and unpacks the reflections of artists to reveal their working practices and illuminate her main concerns: to examine the nexus between the discipline of dance, the interdisciplinary nature of dance-making, and the generative contribution made by movement practices to the development of interdisciplinary performance more generally. The great strength of this section of the essay is the way her analysis of what artists do and say offers explanation of, and potential solace to, the nagging concern that many dance makers have with regard to the disciplinary and social relevance of their work. I would very much like to see Erin expand this avenue of reflection over the coming years: it reveals a great deal not only about how dancers conduct embodied research, but also how they might think about the nexus between the discipline and interdisplinarity.

I particularly agree with Erin when she states: 'While there has been much discussion about interdisciplinarity in dance theory, it is ironic—and surprising—that there has been so little about the creative operations of interdisciplinary practice' (p.25). Ironic, yes, but perhaps not all that surprising. Academics have often been guilty of speaking of and to a performance practice without a sense of obliged recourse to the ideas and articulations of those who create those performances. Erin has always had a clear understanding of the potential for revelatory reflections, and the obligation to seek such reflections from those engaged in choreographic practices who are essentially, as she makes clear, engaged in practice-based research processes.

There are some great moments in this essay, particularly when Erin frames and then unpacks the words of the artists she has chosen to assist her in the investigation of the relationships between what is specific to dance and what is inherently and potentially interdisciplinary about the form. For example, she describes Helen Herbertson's *Sunstruck*, simply and succinctly, and then quotes Helen herself: 'I know its strange and it's not a story and there's not a huge amount to hang on to, but if you can come to it, then you can really get a lot out of it.' Erin then unpacks this by asserting that 'the moving body can often leave little to "hang on to"' but this 'seems to be the strength of this kind of work: a performance event that is based on the deep complexity of the moving bodies [...] but expands to say something about human relationships' (p. 33).

Although Erin is aware of the manner in which dance artists have engaged with contemporary theory in their development of performance work—particularly with the move to 'conceptual dance'—here she highlights the manner in which breach, crisis and resolution have been identified and dealt with within choreographic composition, which then 'forces the shift in theory and criticism' (p.26). This is an important distinction, and it is made possible by Erin's concentration on what dance practitioners do and what they say about what they do.

The essay is not about all dance work at all times. Ultimately its aim is to invigorate a discussion about dance that negotiates a 'path between an overtly interdisciplinary approach to the *mise en scène* and a commitment to choreographic research and craft' (p.26). But, for Erin, it is not enough simply to reverse the usual hierarchy, as so often happens in academic writing, where the choreography becomes 'the dominating force that calls all the other elements of the *mise en scène* to order' (p.27). Instead, she argues for an '"unhierarchized" heterogeneity', a much more useful (if less comfortable) position from which to explore the relationship between disciplines and interdisciplinarity.

I was very satisfied by the first forty pages of this essay. However, its final section, 'Training future dance artists', caused me some frustration. So successfully had Erin identified a lack of discussion around 'the creative operations of interdisciplinary practice' and, coupled with her insightful unpicking of this apparent lack through an exploration of the 'compositional labour of interdisciplinarity in contemporary dance' (p.51), that I hoped she would end by proposing some kind of resolution. Instead I was disappointed that she wanted to discuss the state of tertiary institutional practices in this country.

Reading these last pages made me wonder why so many of us (myself included) return, again and again, to the question of institutional training. Of course, we are concerned with ways in which we can help dance flourish with/without/within the institutions that we have/do not have and what their relevance is to the development of dance in more public forums and in relation to other art forms. Erin might have been better advised to leave this discussion to the Elizabeth Dempster paper from which she quotes, or to others who have discussed this problem before her. The essay should perhaps have ended by pointing to some resolution of the important process that the discussion had instigated, a process I believe has the potential to help resolve all those idiosyncratic disturbances that see so many dance makers hovering on the brink of distrust—concerned with the revelation and recognition of relevance for and within their discipline, but also drawn, if Erin is correct, to the inevitability of their interdisciplinarity.

But it may well be impossible to avoid the subject of dance in tertiary education in NSW, when we are given licence to 'talk' about dance in a public forum. As Erin reminds us, there has been a slash-and-burn process at work in this state over the last 15 years. I wouldn't like to count how many times members of the dance community have been called upon to argue for the development, redevelopment, redeployment or demise of dance (and other performance-directed courses) in the NSW-based tertiary system.

Indeed, I note with surprise, regret (and irony) that another such occasion has arisen. The publication of Erin Brannigan's essay coincides with the announcement that the University of NSW will not appoint to the new senior position in Dance at the School of English, Media and Performing Arts. The school/university administration are backing away from their former commitment to de-velop dance at the Kensington Campus. Instead of being expanded and/or complemented, the Dance Education program is to be phased out—with the promise of yet more consultative talks about the form the teaching of dance might take at the University of NSW by 2012. Mmmm, where have I heard this before? Perhaps it was as the University of Western Sydney's Dance program, followed by its Acting program, slowly crumbled to dust after years of consultative processes? Of course, all institutions have the right to explore a variety of avenues in order to develop new structures that are relevant to the its local, national and international profile and, as they try once again to get it right, I wish the staff at the University of NSW the best of luck.

I hope, however, that, as the powers-that-be once again examine what their Dance program may or may not be, they take heed of what I regard as the most in-novative and constructive section of Erin Brannigan's Platform Paper. As she reminds us, when she returns to her main argument at the end, the artists she talks about—Helen Herbertson, Gideon Oberzanek, Lucy Guerin, Tess de Quincey, Narelle Benjamin, Ros Chrisp,

Julie-Anne Long, Nalina Wait, Sue Healey (and she could have added many others) are 'living proof' that dance (disciplined, undisciplined and interdisciplinary) begins with 'somatic, embodied knowledge and intense physical training' (p.46) in no particular, but very specific, forms of movement practice. The important thing, as Lucy Guerin says, is not the kind of practice practised, but that whatever it is should be an 'intense and defined and articulate physical practice'. At this point the essay is consistent with, or at least returns to, its primary (and, to my mind, most interesting) theme: an exploration of the 'compositional labour of interdisciplinarity in contemporary dance and what this labour might reveal in favour of *the choreographic* as a body of knowledge that exceeds its disciplinary parameters' (p.51, emphasis in original). I can only encourage Erin to continue—to use her skills as researcher and writer to explore this 'compositional labour' of contemporary dance in the company of practitioners, as she has done so eloquently in *Moving Across Disciplines: Dance in the Twenty-first Century*.

Julie-Anne Long is an independent dance artist based in Sydney. She is currently Dance Curator at Campbelltown Arts Centre and has recently completed a PhD in the School of English, Media and Performing Arts at The University of New South Wales.

Erin Brannigan's deeply considered *Moving across Disciplines* highlights the centrality of the art form of dance and the role played by dance artists in interdisciplinary, multidisciplinary and hybrid performance work. Her initial focus is on interdisciplinary performance outcomes, and offers excellent case studies that place Australian dance artists working across multidisciplinary practices in both a historical and contemporary international context. But it is in the final section of the essay that she reveals what in her view is most at stake. Here she turns to questions of dance training and, more specifically, the unstable state of, and inadequate opportunities for, tertiary dance training in New South Wales.

My own experience of tertiary dance training began in 1980, when I crossed the Tasman with a Solo Seal (the final ballet exam of the Royal Academy of Dancing) tucked under my belt to continue my formal training for a further three years at the Victorian College of the Arts, School of Dance. Initially I pursued my Betty Bun-Head dreams, but within a short time turned my attentions to the aspirations of a contemporary dancer. Following graduation I worked for two years in Canberra as a dancer with Human Veins Dance Theatre and in 1985 I moved to Sydney to take up a full-time contract as dancer/choreographer with Kai Tai Chan and the One Extra Company. The way to become a dancer is by 'doing', and in those days 'doing' was possible as fulltime, paid engagement. For the past twenty-five years I have survived through many different incarnations as a dancer, choreographer, performer, maker, teacher, mentor, curator and administrator. I currently call myself 'an independent dance artist'.

However, the performance work I currently make, and have been making for some time, does not utilise in any very obvious way the traditional classical and modern dance languages to which my early years were devoted. For the past decade reviewers have asked of my work: 'Why does she need dancers to do this?' and 'Is this really dance?' To which I reply: 'Why does it matter?' I am a dancer—once a dancer, always a dancer—I think choreographically, and the memory in and of my body, although not explicitly evident, is shaped by more than thirty years of dance training. It's not something of which I want to rid myself. In fact, I am proud of the discipline of dance that has made and continues to make me who I am. My body's history is crucial to the way I currently work as an artist and my dance training has provided me with a strong base from and against which to push. This dance legacy provides me with confidence in the execution of my craft, although from time to time it does make me anxious. Which brings me to what I see is the most urgent provocation of Brannigan's paper.

In light of the recent news that the University of New South Wales is reconsidering plans to develop a dedicated dance performance program, this essay, ironically, serves as a timely reminder of the value of the discipline of dance. Even though I have been, and remain, a vocal critic of the idea that in New South Wales we need a tertiary dance course preparing dancers for the profession, I am anxious that the specificities of the discipline of dance, especially dance-training systems and deep somatic knowledge that can only be acquired over many years of practice, will be undermined if dance is hijacked as a tool for other art forms to use in this interdisciplinary world. For me, part of the appeal of the dance landscape in Sydney is its diversity of training systems and the many influences that the professional sector draws from and engages with. However, I believe, as do choreographers Helen Herbertson and Lucy Guerin (quoted in Brannigan's essay), that the trained dancer brings crucial knowledge to choreographic practice and performance outcomes, even when required to execute minimal movement tasks. It is important to acknowledge that the majority of those 'dance/movement' artists who work in New South Wales have extensive training from somewhere else. Although Erin Brannigan's interest is in dance in the context of widespread interdisciplinarity, the message I take from her important essay is something she refers to as 'the bleedin' obvious', namely that 'we can't have interdisciplinarity without disciplinary specificity'.

Elizabeth Dempster is a senior lecturer in Performance Studies at Victoria University, Melbourne, and co-editor of the journal Writings on Dance. A former dancer/choreographer and founding member of Dance Exchange Company, her choreographic work has been presented throughout Australia and at Dance Umbrella, UK.

Erin Brannigan's Platform Paper dares to initiate a long overdue discussion of the role, meaning and character of discipline in dance in contemporary Australia. I say 'dares' because the term 'discipline', especially when it is combined with dance, has the potential to excite powerfully polarized opinion.

The essay moves forward and back around its topic and in its twists and turns it reminds me of the debates about modernism in dance, which so exercised dance scholars during the late 1980s. A particularly vigorous debate between the critics Sally Banes and Susan Manning conducted in the pages of *The Drama Review* turned on the question of dance's apparently anachronistic status in relation to other arts. Did the development of a modernist aesthetic in dance follow the same broad contours as those of other arts in the twentieth century, or had it evolved in an anomalous way? Is modern dance consistent with aesthetic modernism, or has it traced a different historical trajectory? Brannigan's essay similarly engages historically contested terrain.

It opens with a discussion of the rise of interdisciplinary arts practice over the past thirty years and the challenge that this development might present to disciplinary specificity. However, as Brannigan amply demonstrates, in dance, interdisciplinarity and disciplinary specificity are not always, or necessarily, opposed. In the ballet, for example, disciplinary specificity is both guarded and celebrated, and yet in its stage presentation interdisciplinarity is crucial, with the dance but one part of a spectacle integrating music, design and, to a lesser extent, narrative. In contemporary theatrical dance interdisciplinarity does not represent a break with the past, but more of a continuation and adaptation to contemporary circumstances of well-established habits of collaboration and exchange. An art form such as the ballet, which is confident in its disciplinary identity, has little to fear from the 'spectre of interdisciplinarity'. But a dance practice that is less certain of, or else unwilling to, acknowledge its provenance may well struggle to distinguish itself. And it is here that the imprecise, catch-all term 'contemporary dance' is pulled into service. More of that presently.

According to Brannigan—and I agree with her—it is to twentieth-century modern dance that we must look 'to discover the essence of dance as a discipline', because this is the era when dance assumed an autonomy and economy of means, when the 'subject of dance (became) dancing itself'. However, in an essay by Sally Gardner, which Brannigan cites, the argument is persuasively advanced that modern dance is not disciplinary, at least not in the sense that Foucault might use that term. Unlike the discipline of ballet, modern dance is not predicated upon a rationalized technique, a system of generalizable principles or rules; it is not anonymous and unauthored, but is founded upon intimate, intercorporeal and personalized relationships between the dancer and the choreographer. And there's the conundrum: the dance form that might be said to define the identity of a discipline is in very important ways neither disciplinary nor, in all probability, professional either. Furthermore, it is not and never was 'contemporary'. Such a term disguises and confuses the difference between the two primary dance traditions in Western theatre. It also obscures the perhaps uncomfortable fact that there has been no decisive break with the classical legacy in Australia and that modern dance did not and has not developed as a distinct genre in this country. Ballet is our discipline. There, I've said it.

What constitutes disciplinarity in twenty-first-century dance is a subject in urgent need of discussion, with profound implications not only for the profession, but also for educators and audiences. As Brannigan notes, to invoke the interdisciplinary returns us to the disciplinary and, in the context of Australian dance, to a largely unresolved debate about how two aspects of the word 'discipline', understood both as a field of study, and as a regimen, a system of training and control, might be reconciled. In her seminal work *Reading Dancing: Bodies and Subjects in Contemporary American Dance* (1988), Susan Foster writes that 'making a dance and making a dancer are bound together'. It's hardly surprisingly then that there are real challenges facing curriculum designers in university dance departments today. Dance practice entails rigorous processes of body-based artistic inquiry, and engages values that are resistant to institutionalisation and that, I suspect, are incompatible with those of the contemporary university. But that's another story.